THE CREATURE OF LITUYA BAY

RUSTY WILSON

For Richard Henzel

Lituya Bay, part of Glacier Bay National Park in Alaska.

CONTENTS

Introduction   vii

Prologue   1
Chapter 1   5
Chapter 2   11
Chapter 3   18
Chapter 4   23
Chapter 5   27
Chapter 6   33
Chapter 7   38
Chapter 8   44
Chapter 9   48
Chapter 10   51
Chapter 11   55
Chapter 12   60
Chapter 13   65
Chapter 14   70
Chapter 15   74
Chapter 16   78
Chapter 17   83
Epilogue   88

About the Author   93

INTRODUCTION

Greetings, fellow adventurers, to a story unlike any I've ever heard, and I've heard my share, for sure.

As a fishing guide, I have a tradition of having dutch oven dinners on the group's last day out, and my clients have shared lots of great stories around campfires. But this story is actually one I heard at home from a guy named Joe, who's become a good friend.

I would've probably never heard it if my wife Sarah hadn't decided she wanted a nice deck added to our little cabin near Steamboat Springs, Colorado. She knew I was too busy (a nice way of saying I'm not much of a carpenter), so she asked a friend who runs a construction business if he could help.

Seems he was also too busy, but he in turn had a friend visiting from Utah who would gladly do the job. This friend was Joe, and after Joe finished work each evening, we'd invite him in for dinner.

Joe was such an interesting fellow that we'd end up talking into the wee hours. He'd spent years in Alaska and had lots of gripping tales about bears and such.

But one evening, our talk turned to Glacier Bay National Park, a place Sarah and I have both wanted to visit. We asked Joe if he knew much about it, and come to find out, he did—more than he ever wanted to know, he said, especially about a part called Lituya Bay.

He was at first hesitant to tell his story, but we both finally talked him into it, and I was fortunate that he agreed to let me record it for others.

Since most of my stories feature Bigfoot, I've been asked if the "blue creature" Joe encountered was such, and I have to say I don't know, not having seen it myself. But from Joe's description, my guess is that it was indeed one.

In any case, it's a gripping tale, and having seen the newspaper article Joe refers to later on, I know he was indeed lost in that incredible place.

So, sit back with a cup of hot chocolate in a big comfy chair or by a campfire and enjoy. And if you ever go to Glacier Bay, keep your eyes and ears peeled. Who knows what you might encounter?

—Rusty

PROLOGUE

Rusty, I've never told this story to anyone in detail, but if you really want to hear it, I'm willing to dredge it up, though it's kind of long.

It's been quite a few years since it all came down, and I guess I just haven't felt resolved enough with everything until recently to address it. Maybe telling it will help me tie up some loose ends.

But first, a little background. I was 45 at the time, and a life of delusion had finally caught up with me. When I say delusion, let's just say I fell for some things that aren't necessarily true—the first being that there is one person out there for you, a true love kind of thing, a soul mate. I fell for that one hook, line, and sinker, and when my wife left me, I was devastated.

And then there was the job thing. I had this idea that you worked hard and got ahead, and it was that simple. When my construction business fell apart, I didn't understand why, and I thought I was to blame.

It wasn't until later that I found out my foreman had been stealing from me for years. This was, incidentally, the same guy who ran off with my wife and had been my best friend until then.

Because of all this, I lost my ability to trust, and you can't really have a relationship of any kind without trust, not even with a friend. I'd been a happy-go-lucky kind of guy until then and was transformed into a bitter hard-luck pessimist, somebody no one wanted to be around. I could see only the dark side of things.

There's more to the story, and to this day I can't believe that it happened. It was kind of like a country-western song. I lost everything—my wife, my house, my best friend, my truck, my business—everything.

Even my kids turned against me, siding with their mom in the divorce. They were grown by then, but it still really hurt. She turned them against me by telling lies, making up things I'd never done.

And then, to top it all off, they took my one true friend, my good dog Max, saying I was unfit to care for him. I let him go, because I had no place for him to live, as by then I was homeless.

So I guess I actually was unfit, but it was their doing. In some ways, losing Max was the last straw, the thing that finally broke me.

I was living in Anchorage, Alaska, and believe me, that's a hard town in many ways. It's not a place where you want to be homeless, especially in winter.

I know other people have dealt with even harder stuff—death and illness and that kind of thing—but it all made me feel like I needed to shift my way of thinking, that the world wasn't anything like I'd thought it was, that people weren't trustworthy or worthwhile.

I knew I needed to change my life, but by then I just wanted to be free of everything, including the memories.

And so, in a nutshell, one day I had financial security and people who I thought loved me, and then it was all gone. It left me too broken to even want to fight.

I began to think about ending my life, but I didn't want to hurt my kids, so I decided it had to look like an accident.

I started hanging out at the library, researching places I could go to die, dangerous places where it would look like I'd taken one chance too many instead of intentionally killing myself.

And I finally found that place—Lituya Bay—and it wasn't even all that far away, just down in Glacier Bay National Park.

It was so remote no one would ever find me. I didn't even have to think about it—I just knew it was the place.

And so, I did it—I went to Lituya Bay as mentally and emotionally broken as one can be and still be alive. I went to Lituya Bay to die.

I hoped that by going to one of the wildest and most fearsome and remote places in all of North America, the hand of nature would bring me death and the peace I desired.

But instead, I once again found that my preconceptions were wrong. Lituya Bay was not going to let me off that easily.

Once there, I found something else wanted me dead, something that I assumed intended to kill me in the most horrible way imaginable, something that I didn't even know existed.

So, Rusty, here's my story, and I hope you'll find it worth your time.

Given your own experiences, I know that you'll listen with an open mind, unlike some I've told it to.

So, let's begin.

1

I'll never forget flying to the bay, and in retrospect, I feel kind of sorry for the pilot, as he was a really nice guy. You could tell he became more and more concerned about me as the flight went on.

We flew out of the Lake Hood Seaplane Base near Anchorage, and had I been my normal self, I would've been excited and talking up a storm—after all, it was my first float-plane trip into the Alaska wilderness! I'd always wanted to take aerial photos of the incredible Alaskan wilds, back before I had my optimism beat out of me.

I can still hear the pilot's voice as he asked where my gear was. I told him it was already out there, that another plane had flown it in. This was, of course, a lie and made little sense, as normally one would fly their gear out with them to save money.

But I stumbled on, telling my lie, saying I was a geologist going out to do an extended exploration of the area and had already been supplied by another plane.

He seemed to buy my story, and I quickly changed the subject so he wouldn't start asking me geology questions. It was a subject I knew almost nothing about, except what I'd read about Lituya Bay.

The truth was, I hadn't brought any gear, only the clothes I was wearing and a windbreaker with some crackers I'd stuffed into the pockets in case I got air sick. That was it, as I didn't figure I would need much after I died.

I did have my driver's license in my pocket, as I wasn't sure if I would need an ID to board the plane, but that and the crackers were the extent of my possessions. I planned on destroying the license after I got there, as I didn't want anyone to know what had happened to me, though the odds of anyone finding my body would be slim.

Every penny I had went to the plane trip, which wasn't cheap. In fact, I'd hocked my beloved camera, the only thing I still owned, to fly in. Once again, I didn't figure I would need it after I died.

Lituya Bay is south of Anchorage and north of Glacier Bay, and we flew the Alaska coastline to get there. Lituya is actually part of Glacier Bay National Park and Preserve, and I knew I needed a permit to camp there, but I didn't care, for I didn't intend to really camp, and how can you ticket a dead man?

I would also guess that one would need a permit to land a float-plane there, and whether the pilot had one or not, I didn't know, nor did I care.

In any case, it was a magnificent flight over snow-capped peaks that stretched for hundreds of miles, all cradled by immense glaciers, and I recall thinking it was incredible, though none of it meant much to me.

In a different life, I would've been overwhelmed, taking photo after photo, but I'd lost my ability to feel much of anything.

But even with my indifference, I'll never forget my first

sight of Lituya Bay. I couldn't have picked a more beautiful place to die—or a more dangerous setting.

It's an unreal place, and fittingly, the scene of the most unreal happenings. The Tlingit people have been in the area for countless generations, living in the shadows of the glaciers, and the bay is legendary among them, for it's where Kah Lituya, the god of earthquakes, lives.

Lituya is a Tlingit word meaning *the lake within the point*, referring to the fact that the bay is almost closed off by an extended spit.

The bay itself is two miles wide by seven miles long and is quintessential Alaska. High above, though hidden behind other summits, stands Mount Fairweather in all its glory, the highest mountain in British Columbia at 15,325 feet.

Other lesser yet still massive peaks surround Lituya, with Mount Quincy Adams (13,650 feet) and Mount Crillon (12,700 feet) dominating the skyline.

The bay itself is a deep blue fjord that looks like a huge fish on its side, its flat tail made up of the ice-filled Gilbert Inlet to the north and the Crillon Inlet to the south.

Lituya Bay resembles a huge fish with glaciers for a tail. Cenotaph Island is its eye, and its mouth opens onto the Gulf of Alaska.

The inlets follow the trench of the very active Fairweather Fault and are fed by the Lituya and North Crillon glaciers that sit high near Mount Fairweather.

From the air, I could see that the ice in the inlets was a dirty brown, and I knew from my research that this was landslide debris, for Lituya Bay has seen many large earthquakes.

Looking at the bay from above, the fish's head points towards the turbulent waters of the Gulf of Alaska, with La Chaussee Spit nearly closing the bay off, its narrow entrance having a depth of only 33 feet.

It's a deadly channel at any time besides slack high tide,

and even then, one has to know where to navigate to miss the many boulders and not be swept into the rocks.

To put it mildly, the bay has a reputation, as well as a violent and tumultuous past, not just because of its dangerous entrance, but also from landslides and huge tsunami waves that have periodically scoured the bay's flanks to unbelievable heights.

The lines of destruction were easy to see from the plane, as entire mountainsides had fallen, and also visible were the scour lines of the giant waves.

In 1958, a huge earthquake caused a landslide that resulted in a tsunami that reached up the mountainside to a height of 1,720 feet, sweeping away the forest like matchsticks. Three boats were in the bay that day with six people, four who miraculously escaped, but two who were lost.

But back to the bay's fish shape—its eye would be Cenotaph Island, an almost triangular piece of land bounded on its southern end by steep cliffs filled with colonies of black-legged kittiwakes that seemed to endlessly wheel and glide around the rocks.

Seeing it from the air, I had no idea how important the island would become to me as future events unfolded.

We'd been dropping slowly for some time, and now, as the plane quickly lost altitude, I suddenly had a sense of foreboding.

It seemed natural that I would feel this upon seeing the place I'd chosen for my own death, but I could tell the pilot was feeling it also, for he quickly had the plane on the water and seemed antsy to be rid of me and get going.

We were near Three Saints Point, a location I'd picked along the bay because it was only a little over a half-mile across to Cenotaph Island.

Why that mattered I didn't know, but I would later

realize that my subconscious must've felt the island might come in handy, primarily because I'd read there was an old hermit's cabin there.

"Don't get your feet wet," the pilot said as he edged the plane up to the beach. "We're close enough you can jump if you time it just right."

I thanked him for the ride and grabbed the strut, lowering myself onto the pontoon, waiting for the small waves to retreat. Just before I jumped, the pilot said, "Watch out for brown bears. I've been told this place is crawling with them. Good luck."

I jumped, barely missing the water and sinking into the sand, regaining my balance in time to watch the pilot turn the plane and begin his takeoff.

I stood for a long time after the plane was gone, long after I could hear its engine fading into the distance, wondering how I could have been so stupid.

Finally, I was at the place I'd chosen to end it all, but I now had no idea how I would actually take my own life, and death by bear wasn't on my list.

I realized I hadn't really thought it out very well, and now there would be no going back.

2

I sat on the rocky beach of Lituya Bay for a long time, watching the waves break against the shore of nearby Cenotaph Island.

Hills rose behind me, and I knew they cradled Fish Lake. Purple lupine lined the demarcation between beach and forest.

The beach was littered with the remains of trees uprooted by the giant 1958 tsunami. These, along with numerous rocks, made walking the beach difficult, every step an invitation to a twisted ankle.

It was a pleasant day, and I knew the sun would be up for a long time, as it was late July, and I was in the Land of the Midnight Sun.

I could sit for hours, contemplating my situation, then curl up on the beach and sleep until the sun rose again in the early morn, then sit and contemplate some more.

There was only one problem with this plan—I needed to carry on and die before I got too hungry.

I could already feel my stomach tighten, as I'd been too

despondent to want breakfast earlier. Like death by bear, death by starvation wasn't on my list.

I took the crackers from my pocket. At this point, the words *Premium Saltine* were the only proof I had that civilization even existed, other than my clothes and the ID still in my pocket—and a few fillings in my teeth.

For all I knew, my life had been a dream, and I'd actually been raised by wolves.

I wanted to eat the crackers, but I knew I might find a better use for them later as some kind of bait. I knew they wouldn't work for fishing, as they would dissolve, but maybe some other critter could be lured into reach of the crumbs.

I doubted if I would have it in me to kill anything, even if I were starving, but I put the little packs back into my pocket. Oddly enough, I wasn't even aware that I'd started feeling that I might not want to die after all.

I watched as a gull floated through the air, pausing to look at the strange human creature below on the beach. Circling and passing over me several times, it finally flew towards Cenotaph Island, leaving its sharp call on the wind.

My thoughts turned to wolves—did they come here to the bay? It seemed probable, as they lived almost everywhere else in Alaska. Would I die by wolf?

It seemed improbable, as wolves generally leave humans alone, though it wouldn't be unheard of for a pack to feast on my body—preferably once it was lifeless.

So, here I was, finally at Lituya Bay, hungry and still alive. Soon I would be thirsty, and then what would I do?

I wasn't terribly worried, as I knew there were a multitude of streams that fed water into the bay from the glaciers high above, but that was on the other end of the bay.

If I became too weak from hunger to find water, I could very easily die of dehydration, and vice versa.

I picked up a stick and wrote in the sand:

1. Bear
2. Wolf
3. Starvation
4. Thirst

For some reason, none of these seemed like ways I wanted to die.

But what other ways were there out here? I was sure many more existed, but at the time, starvation seemed the most likely, given the state of my stomach.

Once again taking the crackers from my pocket, I stared at them. What the heck, life's short, especially mine, I mused, opening the packs and slowly eating each cracker, letting them melt in my mouth one by one.

Hopefully I could find something for a main course later, enough to last until I died.

I tossed the cellophane wrappers into the air, where they floated on the wind, taking them towards the glaciers at the end of the bay.

Maybe some mountain climber would find them on top of Mount Fairweather and wonder where they came from, I thought, feeling slightly guilty at adding my two bits' worth of pollution to the pristine landscape, even though I'd read that gold miners had left all kinds of junk here in the late 1800s.

Later, I wondered if those same wrappers hadn't been partly what announced to the bay that a stranger had arrived.

I began slowly walking the beach, trying to regain my sense of equilibrium, as well as to stave off the hunger pangs.

I'd been hungry before, and I knew that after a few days one goes into a sort of numbness and the discomfort lessens, replaced by weakness.

But thirst is different, it gets more and more excruciating with time.

Worried about spraining my ankle, I again sat on a log. I was frustrated, for I didn't want to be around long enough to worry about starvation or dehydration or any of the longer-term ways of dying.

I just needed to get on with it and figure out how to die now. Maybe I should swim into the bay and let myself drown.

I scratched into the sand:

5. Drowning

So far, number five sounded best.

I continued to sit on the huge log, one I guessed had been wrenched off the mountainside by the incredible 1958 tsunami. Maybe I'd get lucky and there would be an earthquake.

I again scratched in the sand:

6. Tsunami

This was my new favorite, but it seemed even more unlikely than the second one, death by wolf.

I leaned back, watching a raven dive from high above to sit on a nearby rock, where it watched me watching it.

Soon, several others circled overhead, and before long more had joined until it was a conspiracy of ravens, all making as much noise as possible.

It was time to go. I'd heard many times about ravens

alerting large predators to nearby prey. It was a symbiotic relationship that allowed them to feast on leftovers, and I had no intention of being anyone's leftovers.

The sun was now getting low in the sky—I was at latitude 58 degrees north, a mere 8 degrees short of the arctic circle, and in summer the arctic twilight lasted for hours. The sun hung low on the horizon, giving everything a dreamy quality.

I was getting chilled and needed to find a place to spend the night, or at least to hide out until I could clear my mind enough to decide the best way to die.

I walked away from the beach and into the edge of a thick forest of Western hemlock and Sitka spruce, the trunks covered with lichens and mosses.

The trees didn't look all that old, and I suspected I was in one of the areas that had been scoured clean by the tsunami, the forest only recently beginning to recover.

Beneath the trees was a thick layer of vegetation made of fungi, liverworts, and wildflowers. I knew that the temperate rainforests of southeast Alaska had some of the largest accumulations of organic material on earth.

The forest shadows were dark and foreboding, but a small trickle of water reflected enough light to catch my eye, and it was there that I drank until I was full.

I sighed—I'd staved off number four, death by thirst or dehydration, at least for now.

And as I crouched in the deep shade of the spruce, I felt something I hadn't felt for years, a sense of hope and promise—not *much* hope and promise, mind you—but enough to give me pause.

I'd looked to nature before for healing, back at other times when I'd had problems, but this time I'd been too far gone to even consider its therapeutic properties—or had I?

Maybe my plan to come to Lituya Bay was a subconscious desire to immerse myself into the only thing I had left, the healing power of the natural world.

If this were true, I wished now my subconscious would've at least thought to bring along a little gorp or trail mix.

It was now getting chilly enough that I knew I needed to do something. Since I had no way to make a fire, I decided my only other choice was to burrow deep into the damp wood duff, much like a bear would do, down under the detritus that covered the forest floor.

Hopefully the layer of pine needles, stems, and bark would be dryer the deeper I dug and act as a blanket, getting me through the cold night. I knew my waterproof jacket would keep me fairly dry.

I dug until I reached dry duff, then crawled into the hole and pulled as much of the organic matter back over me as I could, pulling my hood up around my head.

Hunkering down, I tried to sleep, though my mind was racing like that cacophony of ravens.

Maybe I didn't want to die after all. Unfortunately, it was now probable that I had no choice.

I was totally unprepared for any kind of survival, and I had no knowledge of edible plants nor any way to signal anyone, even if someone did happen to fly over.

The poem, "The Spell of the Yukon," by Robert Service ran through my head. My high-school English teacher had been an adventurer at heart, and Service was one of his favorites, so we read many of his poems.

I wasn't in the Yukon, but it really wasn't all that far away as the crow flies, and part of the poem seemed fitting:

It's the great, big, broad land 'way up yonder,

It's the forests where silence has lease;
It's the beauty that thrills me with wonder,
It's the stillness that fills me with peace.

It was indeed still, and after some time, I began to warm up. I thought about Anchorage, how its noise and human despair contrasted with this quiet landscape, and I soon began to drift off, wishing I was eating pizza at the Moose's Tooth Pub near what had once been my home.

I soon fell into a restful dreamless sleep, cradled by soft needles of Sitka spruce, far from those who wished me harm.

I had no idea that it would be the only night at Lituya Bay that I would sleep soundly, and that soon the desire for death would be replaced by the fear of death, a fear that would become my constant and unwelcome companion.

Unknown to me, the ravens had indeed alerted the bay to my presence, and a new enemy had awakened, one I never imagined could even exist.

3

I woke to find myself shrouded in fog. Above me, the tree trunks disappeared into gray shadows, and looking out to the bay, I could see tendrils of mist floating over the calm water.

I dug myself out of the duff, my stomach feeling like I'd been punched—I was hungry, but I knew I would find no relief, at least not here.

I had absolutely no knowledge of edible plants, and I was more likely to be eaten than to eat. As for fishing, I had nothing to fish with except my bare hands.

I slowly walked to the beach, where a touch of reality greeted me in the form of huge bear tracks in the sand. I recalled the words of the pilot and knew he was right, that there had to be brown bears here.

It was a great habitat for them, and I was looking directly at proof that one had walked within a hundred feet of my bed during the night. Bears have incredible senses of smell, so surely it had known, or had the duff covered my scent?

Of all the ways to die, death by bear had to be the worst,

primarily because they don't necessarily make sure you're dead before they start feasting on you.

It was a depressing thought, and I was suddenly aware that the knot in my stomach wasn't just from hunger, but also from fear.

I realized I was in plain sight on the beach and felt the immediate need to remedy that, but I didn't really feel safe going into the shadowy forest where I couldn't see around me. But with the thick fog, it was hard to see more than a few hundred feet, so it was unlikely anyone could see me.

Even if there were bears in the area, they might smell me, but I would probably see them first. Bears have poor eyesight, relying more on their sense of smell.

I suddenly longed for a kayak or some means of going out on the water. I knew brown bears were good swimmers, but I'd never heard of one trying to kill someone while swimming. It seemed like it would be hard to do and wouldn't be one of their preferred ways of getting lunch.

But most bears weren't interested in humans, and I knew I was more likely to scare them off than be attacked. So, instead of hiding in the forest, I sat again on the large log on the beach. The fog seemed to be slowly lifting.

Looking towards Cenotaph Island, I could barely make out the dark forest through the mists. Were there bears on the island? I was sure there had to be, as it wouldn't be hard for one to swim out there. Would I be safer if I could somehow get there? Could I find water?

I recalled reading about a hermit who had lived on the island, built a cabin, and improved a spring, the only water there.

Maybe I could float on a log and get there, but what good would that do? My immediate need was for food, and why was I so sure I would be safer on Cenotaph?

The name Cenotaph added to the gloom of the fog, for it means *empty tomb*. The island had been named in 1768 by Jean-Francios de Laperouse, a French explorer, after he'd lost 21 men in the entrance to the bay when their ships sank.

My endless research on Lituya Bay had dredged up numerous such stories of death and disaster—21 French, nine Russians, over 150 Tlingits, and a number of American sailors had all died trying to enter the bay.

This was part of the reason why I'd chosen this place to die. I would be in good company.

As the morning wore on and my stomach felt emptier, I knew something had changed. I seemed to have become more focused on my immediate need for food instead of dying. Something was beginning to awake inside me.

I made my way down the rocky beach, watching for some kind of sea life that might have washed up on shore. Maybe I would find a crab or small fish that had been brought in on the tide.

I didn't want to go far, but stay close to my duff bed and small stream, for they offered the only comfort I found in this huge landscape.

Something soon caught my eye—a gull's nest in the rocks holding three beautiful pale-green eggs with dark-green splotches.

I knew the Tlingit ate gulls' eggs, as I'd recently read an article in the Anchorage paper where Glacier Bay National Park was going to allow the Tlingit to again gather eggs in the park as part of their traditional harvest.

I bent down to pick one up, then hesitated. As hungry as I was, the thought of eating raw eggs was unappealing. But knowing they were there if I couldn't find anything else was comforting—that is, until I thought of yet another way to die.

I picked up a stick and scratched in the sand:

7. Salmonella

If the eggs weren't fresh, food poisoning would be a most uncomfortable way to go. What I didn't know at the time was that gulls typically lay their eggs in late May, and these eggs had been abandoned. Since it was now July, odds were good they were inedible.

That nest ended up having the only eggs I saw while at Lituya.

I now examined a plant that looked a lot like parsley, breaking off a small part and tasting it.

It was indeed wild parsley, and I could add it to my list of potential foods, though I wasn't hungry enough yet that it sounded good. I picked some and stuffed it in my pocket.

The fog had lifted, and I could make out the summits of massive peaks far above the east end of the bay, the sky behind them a pale blue.

Scanning the landscape, something now caught my eye, a patch of pink near the forest. I figured it must be fireweed, which is edible, so I trudged over to take a look.

When I got there, I realized I'd finally found something even better—wild strawberries! And as I ate my fill and stuffed even more into my jacket pockets, I wondered if the salmon might not soon come into the bay, as the run should be starting. If I could survive until then, I'd be in sushi heaven.

Later, after I'd once again drank my fill of the clear water from the little stream and buried myself deep in the duff, I thought about how, not more than 24 hours before, I'd come to Lituya Bay to die.

Now, my stomach full of wild strawberries and wild

parsley, I felt something I hadn't felt for years—a sense of pride, for I'd managed to survive a full day here.

I was still hungry, but the edge was gone, and I knew I had a chance at surviving, though maybe not a good one.

I knew my life was still on the line, for winter comes early to the coastal bays and mountains of Alaska, and I knew there was no way I could survive the bitter cold here.

But maybe, just maybe, if I could continue to feed myself, someone would eventually come into the bay and I could go back out with them. I suspected the Tlingit still fished here occasionally, as it was part of their traditional territory.

As I lay there under the big trees, I wondered where I would go if I were rescued. I knew it wouldn't be Anchorage, except to get Max.

Maybe I would return to my childhood home in the little high-desert town of Sunnyside, Utah, where my grandparents had settled from Tennessee, my grandpa and dad both becoming coal miners.

I had no idea what I would do in Utah, as the coal mines were fading into oblivion, but the thought gave me great comfort as I drifted off in my warm pine-needle bed.

I slept like a baby, totally unaware that I was now, thanks to the ravens, on the radar of a creature who felt nothing but anger at my intrusion.

4

Something woke me, but I wasn't sure what. All I knew was that it was still dark, which meant that it had to be sometime between about midnight and three a.m., as that was the only time it was ever really dark this far north in the summer.

My first thought was that there'd been an earthquake. I lay very still, but didn't hear the sound of rocks clattering down the mountainsides, which would surely happen during an earthquake.

Suddenly, I again felt that same strange sense of foreboding that I'd felt on the plane. It's hard to explain, but it was kind of a feeling of doom combined with a fear of the supernatural, like being up against something you can't touch or see or wrap your mind around. It was a helpless and terrifying feeling.

I'd read of others who'd had the same feeling in the bay —explorers, climbers, and geologists. The Tlingits regarded the place with great trepidation.

I'd personally always felt there are things that we can't know, things we don't know, and things we don't want to know. Maybe a sense of foreboding tells us we're dealing with something we're better off not knowing.

As I lay there in the dark, surrounded by the pleasant smell of pine needles, completely buried except for my face, the feeling of dread increased until it was all I could do to keep myself from getting up and fleeing. The fact that I had nowhere to flee to was the only thing that kept me still.

It was then that I thought more deeply about those things we don't want to know, for far in the distance I could hear something screaming—no, not screaming, but more of a howling.

I ran through a list in my mind of all the things it could possibly be—moose, wolf, bear, mountain lion, or even a whale out in the bay, but I knew it was none of these.

Whatever it was, it was far away, and it had to be something large to make a sound that could carry like that. It had to be something with a huge torso to hold large powerful lungs, for the sound went on and on until I marveled that whatever it was didn't stop to catch its breath.

In addition, the sound wavered up and down like a siren, undulating like a wave. I had never in my wildest dreams heard anything even vaguely like it, and it made the hair on my neck stand up.

There was literally nothing I could do but lie as still as possible and hope this creature didn't know I was there. It seemed far enough away that I was safe, but had it seen me down on the beach or picking strawberries? What in hells-bells was it, anyway?

I began to shake, but not because I was cold. For some reason, the cry had pushed me to the very edge of terror, much more so than any thoughts of being eaten by a grizzly.

In retrospect, I think it was because it seemed so foreign, like something from another dimension, something completely removed from the world I knew, and thereby something that didn't follow the same physical laws. But what could it be?

I forced myself to take deep breaths, calming myself until I finally stopped shivering.

I'd read that humans, like other mammals, release a fear pheromone in our sweat when we're stressed that can be detected by humans as well as by animals. If we're in a predator-prey situation, the predator can sense our fear, giving it an advantage.

I knew it was critical to my survival to relax, but how could anyone not be afraid of a scream like that? And it was so far away, how could it know I was afraid? I doubted it would be able to smell the pheromones from such a distance. It sounded like it was way up at the end of the bay, maybe even up on Lituya Glacier.

But even if the creature couldn't sense my fear, a nearby bear surely could, and I had to do something to calm myself down.

I found it ironic that I was now afraid of dying when I'd come here for that express purpose. In fact, my will to live seemed to be getting stronger with every hour I was out here.

I began thinking of Max, of his big dark eyes set in his golden retriever face, giving him a look of being wise beyond his years. He was the best dog I'd ever had, and I suddenly missed him terribly. I felt alone and empty.

How could I have let my ex-wife take him? I truly believed I was doing the right thing by leaving him, that I couldn't take care of him, but I now realized those thoughts, those deep insecurities, had been put into my head.

She knew how much I loved the dog, and it was her ultimate thrust into my heart to see me freely give him up. I wondered if she were even taking care of him, as he'd always been my dog, and she'd never paid him much attention.

I began softly sobbing, even though I knew I might attract a bear—or worse. I think I'd been in denial until then, and as I became more and more awake to all the pain I'd gone through, I began to realize that killing myself would have made my ex-wife happy.

It was a difficult thing to come to grips with, the fact that someone you loved and who once claimed to love you could be so cruel, but that night there at Lituya Bay, something in the depth and horror of that distant call shook me from my waking nightmare.

It was ironic that the deepest fear imaginable had in turn awakened something primal in me, something that wanted very much to live.

I dried my eyes with the back of my hand and settled down deeper into the duff, vowing that no matter what, I would return to Anchorage and get Max.

I didn't know what creature could've made that fearsome call, but I did know that neither it nor anything else would stop me. I would leave Lituya Bay alive. Together, somehow, Max and I would start a new life down in a quiet little town in Utah.

I soon drifted back off, finally relaxing, my determination giving me new hope.

5

I was again awakened, but this time not by a distant howl, but by something shuffling nearby.

My instinct was to cover my face, and I slowly and quietly pulled matted leaves and needles over my head, except for my nose and eyes.

Whatever it was, it was big, and my first impression was that it was a brown bear, as no black bear could carry that much weight.

I knew it was heavy because I could actually feel it sinking into the duff with each step. It actually seemed beyond heavy, almost ponderous.

If it were a brown bear, I was sure it would soon find me through its sense of smell. I waited, holding my breath, trying not to be afraid. The last thing I wanted to do was release fear pheromones that would lead it directly to me.

I remembered something my son Mark had told me. It was my 40th birthday, and he'd purchased a paraglider ride for me up at Hatcher Pass out of Palmer, near Anchorage.

He was so excited that I couldn't tell him I was afraid of

heights, so I just gritted my teeth and decided to go along for the ride, no matter what.

But once there, I was having second thoughts and had pretty much decided to bail, and Mark could see I was afraid.

He said, "Dad, don't think about it, just go to your happy place."

"What's a happy place?" I asked.

"It can be anywhere you want it to be," he answered. "It's just some place you go to take your mind off whatever you're afraid of."

At the time, I'd pretty much forgotten what it meant to be happy, but I did enjoy hiking in Chugach Park with Max, so I decided to make that my happy place.

So, as the instructor and I took those first few running steps together off the pass in the tandem paraglider, I closed my eyes and thought of hiking with Max. Once up into the air, I forgot my fears and was instead filled with exhilaration and excitement.

It was a ride I never forgot, nor did I forget Mark's advice about going to your happy place when you're afraid or depressed.

OK, so if I were attacked by this bear or whatever it was, I figured I would try to make my final thoughts be happy ones of hiking with Max, watching as he bounced along the trail with that carefree silliness only a golden retriever can have.

But even thoughts of Max weren't enough to distract me as the thing came closer. I could no longer hold my breath, so I breathed as slowly and quietly as possible, afraid to open my eyes.

It felt as if it were now standing directly over me. Whatever it was, it had discovered where I was hiding, and I steeled myself for whatever horrible thing might come next.

But nothing happened. It had to be waiting for me to move, maybe so it could determine exactly where I was. If I radiated fear, I knew it would find me.

Unbelievably, I relaxed and felt myself go into a state that almost seemed like hibernation. I could feel my pulse slowing, and it felt as if my blood was barely flowing through my veins.

After what seemed like forever, I could again hear footsteps, and whatever it was seemed to be leaving.

Apparently, it hadn't smelled me, which was puzzling, for bears have long snouts which give them a sense of smell that's much better than a bloodhound's. Maybe being buried in the forest debris had masked my scent.

I was soon overcome by a powerful stench, and it was all I could do to not cough or gag. Somehow, it seemed like the creature had purposefully released some kind of musk, possibly to get a reaction from me and find where I was hiding. I went again to my happy place, but it was all I could do to breathe.

I wanted to open my eyes and see exactly what I was dealing with, but it occurred to me that perhaps the creature was clever enough to walk away, hoping for exactly such a reaction, but was still watching.

I kept my eyes closed, and something told me I didn't want to know anyway.

Finally, after what seemed like at least an hour, I could stand it no longer and slowly opened my eyes, squinting. The moon was gibbous, and enough light filtered through the trees that I could make out the little sparkling stream not far from my duff nest. Whatever it was seemed to have gone.

Because my bed was on the edge of the forest, I could see down to the beach by raising my head. The bay shimmered in the moonlight, and I remember thinking it was the most ethereal thing I'd ever seen. It struck me that I was truly in the heart of some of the most beautiful and amazing wilderness on the planet.

It was then that I made out some kind of form walking in the distance. I shivered, for whatever it was, it was huge.

But what really gave me pause was its color. I know some bears can have a light brown tawny coat, but this creature looked to be almost a powder blue-gray.

Either the moonlight was playing a trick on my eyes, or I was looking at a huge glacier bear. Glacier bears are sometimes called blue bears for their silver-blue hair. They're a subspecies of black bear, and it's believed that their silver-blue color is an adaptation to life on and around glaciers. They're found only in the southeast Alaska and British Columbia mountains and forests.

If it was a glacier bear, it was particularly fearsome, I thought, being so big. But the wild and uncontrollable fear I felt told me it was no bear, but something else, something almost unfathomable to my puny human brain.

As I watched, the creature slowly walked along the edge of the waters, seemingly paying no mind to the rocks that had made such slow going for me, almost as if floating above them.

It turned and looked back towards me, and I instinctively lowered my head and closed my eyes. When I opened them it was gone, like a ghost.

I was shivering again. I decided that there were two problems here, the first being that I'd never heard of any kind of bear being that large, except for maybe the Kodiak bear, which, with the polar bear, shares the distinction of being the largest bear on earth.

Maybe a Kodiak had somehow swam into the bay and taken up residence. It wouldn't be impossible, given the range that bears have, even though Kodiak Island was over 600 miles away.

The second problem, one I couldn't easily explain, was that the bear was upright, walking on two legs, just like a human.

I lay still, thinking, and it occurred to me that there was a third problem—the problem of my fears.

I'd never felt anything like this, and I'd been in close range of bears before. My fears were more as if I'd seen a ghost, an alien, and a dire bear all wrapped up in one creature.

I knew the sun would soon be up, for I could now make out the first hint of dawn in the sky above the bay. I wanted to get up and flee, but once again, I had nowhere to go, and doing so would without doubt put me in even greater danger.

I again closed my eyes. In my mind's eye, I picked up a stick and wrote yet another way to die in Lituya Bay:

8. Strange creature

I knew that the sooner I could leave the bay the better— even a single day might make the difference between life and death. It was an undeniable fact that whatever this was, it was searching for me, and I had a bad feeling about what it would do when it actually found me. The scream I'd heard coming from far away on the glacier was filled with anger and hatred.

I had seen no boats come into the bay since I'd arrived,

and a rescue didn't seem forthcoming, so I knew I had no choice but to somehow get away from this thing on my own.

The only way I knew to do that was to get to Cenotaph Island and not be seen doing it. I could then hide there until someone came along in a boat or I figured out some other way to escape.

But it was a task I was pretty sure I wasn't up to.

6

The first thing I did after crawling from my nest was to go fill my stomach with water from the little stream.

Doing so would help stop the hunger pangs, as well as keep me hydrated until I could find another water source, for I knew I had to find a new place to sleep.

The creature had almost stumbled upon me, and I was sure it would be back. It was likely it had seen me go into the woods the previous evening.

The next thing I did was take mud from the stream and rub it all over my head and clothes. Fortunately, my rain jacket was an olive green and didn't stand out much, and my pants were already the color of dirt from sleeping in the duff.

My next task would be to find enough food to get me through the day so I would have enough strength to figure out some kind of boat to take me to the island.

Staying along the edge of the forest, I made my way to the strawberry patch. I would eat as many strawberries as possible and again fill my pockets, and that would at least be a start.

But once there, I was shocked at what I saw. The entire patch was totally destroyed, the berries completely smashed as if huge feet had stomped them into oblivion.

It looked as if very little was salvageable, and I now knew that going out into the open to scavenge would be a big mistake.

I slipped back into the forest shadows and made my way back to my duff nest.

If I were to parallel the forest and go towards the spit, I knew there was a small cove that might hide me. I also knew there was a stream beyond it flowing down from Fish Lake.

The stream was big enough that it could possibly have fish. The only problem with this is that I was getting further from the shores of Cenotaph.

I continued along the forest's edge, slowly making my way, until I finally felt satisfied that I was hidden from view, the beach curving inland.

I then began walking along the bay where I hoped that, with all the dead trees beached from past tsunamis, I might find something that would carry me to the island.

I've read that times of danger make us feel most alive, and I don't think I've ever felt more alive than when I found the tracks in the wet sand. It made me truly understand what it means to feel your heart in your throat.

The tracks were huge and looked nothing like the bear tracks I'd seen, which had claw prints and segmented pads, but rather looked more like a human foot.

It looked as if the creature had come from the forest to the beach, stood there for awhile, then turned and gone back. Had it been watching me?

Putting my own foot inside one of the tracks, I could see that one track would hold two or three of mine, and it also sank much deeper.

I turned, panicked, half expecting to hear the same undulating howl I'd heard before, but the only sound was the wind blowing sand into my eyes. A storm was coming in.

Living in Anchorage, one hears the stories about the Gulf of Alaska and how treacherous it can be, how quickly the high winds can come up and catch boaters unawares.

Looking out past the spit, I could see waves breaking, and I knew the spit would provide some protection, but once the winds really hit, the waves in the bay would become impassable, especially on something like a log. It sounded like yet another way to die.

Picking up a small stick, I scratched in the sand:

9. Wind

I stood there for the longest time, watching the wind blow away not only the giant tracks, but also my scratches in the sand.

I was having an internal debate over whether or not wind qualified as a way to die, or if it really should be listed under drowning.

And as the wind grew stronger, I suddenly realized how weak I'd become.

I hadn't had anything but strawberries, a few crackers, and a handful of wild parsley since arriving at Lituya Bay. At this point, I was becoming disoriented enough that I didn't even know how many days I'd been there.

That mental fuzziness made me indecisive, and I didn't know what to do. Should I continue walking the beach looking for a log that I could hopefully paddle to the island?

The incoming winds made that proposition seem foolish, especially since logs tend to rotate, and I wasn't sure I could stay on one.

But I knew I had to escape, for if the creature returned and found me during the coming night, my indecision would be the least of my problems.

Should I go back into the forest and try to find some edible plants so I could regain my strength? Maybe I could find more strawberries if I kept looking. Without more energy, I wouldn't be able to paddle to the island, even if the winds let up.

Maybe I should try to find Fish Creek, for I would again be needing water at some point. I could dig another nest and hole up there until the storm passed through.

It then occurred to me that rain would turn my comfortable nest into a soggy pit, one that would quickly draw warmth away from me, leaving me hypothermic.

The thought of trying to sleep in a soaking rainforest seemed to galvanize me, and I knew I had to keep walking the beach, looking for something that would serve as a boat.

I desperately needed to go to the island and reach the shelter of the hermit's cabin, assuming it was still there.

As I continued down the rocky beach, looking through the masses of dead trees, I thought back to how badly I'd wanted to die. It now looked as if my wish was going to come true, and it seemed I had no power to stop it, even though I'd now changed my mind.

I tried to think of Max and focus on my happy place, but it wasn't much use, and I slowly fell into a deep pit of despair, barely able to make myself continue along.

I finally reached the cove. Walking around its far side, I spotted a plank so weathered it had turned gray, yet it was still floating and not waterlogged.

It was thick and looked to be made from red cedar, which meant it had been part of a Tlingit dugout canoe that had probably crashed on the spit.

And it was wide enough that I could lie on it and try to paddle my way across the bay—if only I could conjure up the strength before the winds got worse.

I knew I was running out of time.

I had to find Fish Creek and see if it would live up to its name, for I desperately needed something to eat.

7

I stashed the cedar plank safely on shore, then continued along the edge of the trees until I eventually came to a break in the forest.

Sure enough, a small stream flowed there into the bay, and I knew from my earlier research that it was Fish Creek, tumbling down from Fish Lake above.

It was then that I saw the fish. It had started its way up the creek, and as it jumped over a rock, its pink tail announced it was a sockeye.

I knew that sockeye were different from most salmon in that they require a lake for their young, and any river you see sockeye in will lead to a lake.

It surprised me to actually see the fish, as I'd read that Fish Lake had been clogged up with logs and debris from the 1958 tsunami, reducing the salmon population. In addition, sockeye are becoming more and more rare, and if anything, I expected to see a coho.

Regardless, I lunged for the fish, getting wet up to my knees in the cold water. But it was gone, swimming its way upstream, heading for its own birthplace, where it would hatch its eggs and die.

I thought that if I waited long enough, it might come floating back down the stream, dead, and I wouldn't have to kill it. I could just stand there and do nothing but wait. It would make things much easier.

It seemed like the thing to do, until I finally realized how muddled my thinking was becoming, a precursor to bad choices that could eventually kill me.

I needed food now. Besides, the fish was going to a lake and would die there, not float back down the stream.

I quickly sprang into action, running along the bank of the stream, following the salmon. Soon ahead of it, I jumped into the water, miraculously grabbing onto it. It was slippery and fought the good fight, but I had no choice but to kill and eat it.

In retrospect, I felt bad about killing the fish, but after I'd eaten my fill of the pink meat and stuffed the rest into my pocket, I consoled myself by saying I was just another part of nature, of the chain of life.

It didn't take long to feel better, and as I walked back down the edge of the stream, I found a small thicket of blueberries.

I'd taken my kids blueberry picking when they were younger, and I knew to pick those with a light grey-blue color, skipping the red ones, as they weren't ripe and would give you a stomach ache.

I also knew to avoid white berries, as in Alaska, they're all poisonous. The most infamous poisonous berry in Alaska is the baneberry, which has white or red berries. But it tastes so bitter that people usually spit them out before swallowing.

I ate as many blueberries as I could, then stuffed hand-fuls into my pockets, along with the salmon.

As I drank from the stream, I marveled at how quickly my luck had changed. Subsistence living was not for the faint of heart, and I gained a new appreciation for the natives who'd managed to survive for thousands of years in this wild environment.

I also had a new respect for the bears and all the other animals who lived day by day, never knowing where their next meal would come from.

My stomach was full, I had food in reserve, and if I could somehow make it across the bay on that plank, I might just pull off an escape. My determination to get Max back seemed to be about the only thing moving me forward.

Thinking again about what I was escaping from, I felt a sense of urgency. The incoming wind was getting stronger, and I dragged the plank to the water, then slipped onto it much like one would ride a surfboard out to sea, flat on my stomach, paddling with my arms.

It was only a few moments before I slid off, nothing holding me onto the slippery surface. I barely managed to keep the plank from going out to sea.

Back on the beach, I took my jacket off and twirled it into a sort of rope, then tied myself to the plank as tightly as possible, pushing back out into the waves.

I soon had the hang of things, though I almost capsized more than once. But once away from the beach and the breaking waves, things got easier, at least in terms of keeping my balance.

I was soon paddling like a machine, soaking wet and cold, focusing only on the waves and staying afloat as each stroke pushed me closer to Cenotaph Island. The coat was helping, ratcheting my body close to the plank.

I knew that if I crashed, it would be questionable as to whether or not I could swim to shore, as it might be too far for both my strength and swimming abilities.

It seemed the berries had given me a surge of raw energy, for I felt strong and capable, but the further I got from the beach, the more I felt I was relying on the energy from the salmon.

But as the storm came closer, the waves got higher and stiffer, making it difficult to stay on the plank, in spite of the coat. I was beginning to question my ability to reach Cenotaph, even though I could now barely make out the massive form of the island ahead through the spray.

An occasional sea bird winged over to check me out— first a gull, then a kittiwake, then what looked to be the same ravens that had alerted the creature to my presence when I first arrived. I cursed them silently, not wanting to waste the energy it would take to yell.

I was tired. I'd been on the waves for what seemed like forever, and though it had only been a little over a mile out to the island, it seemed much farther.

And now I saw small eyes paralleling me in the water— curious sea otters! There was something about their dark fluid eyes that reminded me of Max, and I felt a new surge of energy.

I had to make it to Cenotaph Island—I had to get Max. Who knew if my ex was even taking care of him?

And again, from nowhere, I recalled the lines of another Robert Service poem I'd learned in high school, "The Call of the Yukon."

> This is the Law of the Yukon, that only the
>   Strong shall thrive,

That surely the Weak shall perish, and only
    the Fit survive.
Dissolute, damned and dispairful, crippled
    and palsied and slain,
This is the Will of the Yukon—Lo! how she
    makes it plain!

Would I end up being one of the weak or one of the strong? It seemed silly, but the mind grabs onto whatever it can when under duress, and I decided I would be one of the strong. I would not only survive, but I would thrive. But for now, mists were rolling in, and where had Cenotaph gone?

And then, out there in the turbulent waters, soaked and barely hanging on, I remembered a new way to die at Lituya.

In my mind's eye, I wrote in the sand:

10. Shark

I'd read that the bay had sharks in the summer when the waters warmed, and they'd been a bane to native and non-native salmon fishermen alike. The Tlingit feared the shark, using the skin for sandpaper and the teeth for necklaces.

I became hyper-aware, every whitecap now looking like a shark's fin. Finally, just as I thought my arms would fall off, I made out hundreds of black-legged kittiwakes circling—I must be close to the shore. Would I actually make it?

I felt a surge of exhilaration as the mists parted and the island looked to be only a few hundred feet away, maybe closer.

It was then I realized I wasn't making any progress.

I groaned. The tide was going out and would take me out to sea, or worse yet, smash me against the rocks. On top of that, I could feel my coat starting to loosen, and it was getting hard to stay on the plank.

Cenotaph, empty tomb—so close and yet so far.

Suddenly, the coat loosened and caught in the wind, billowing out as the plank slipped from beneath me.

Without my weight, the plank took off on the waves like an empty skiff. My jacket caught on my foot for a moment, then slipped away, following the plank—along with the salmon, berries, and my driver's license.

My luck had again changed.

I wanted to cry, but instead, I somehow swam to shore.

8

I lay sprawled on the beach, ecstatic that I'd made it, even though I knew I needed to get up and move around to warm myself.

When you're on the edge, you tend to live moment by moment, just trying to survive, but lying there, my only thought was that I'd made it across the bay and was now on the island, that much closer to getting Max.

In reality, I wasn't any closer to anything. I had no food, and the raw salmon had made my stomach hurt, nor was I sure where to find water. My coat, with what little food I'd had, was gone.

I'd read about a hermit from Ohio named James Huscroft who'd lived at Lituya Bay for many years, eating coho salmon and berries, much as I'd been doing.

He'd built a cabin in 1915 on the island near a spring, where he'd laboriously built up the soil until he had a magnificent garden.

He'd installed an iron pipe to bring the spring water to the garden, and I knew if I could find the pipe, I would also find the spring, assuming it was still active.

But all I knew was that the cabin was on the west side of the island, not far from where I'd just crawled onshore.

I'd come to Cenotaph partly to escape the strange blue creature, but also because I needed shelter from the impending rain. I could no longer sleep in a hole in the forest duff. It was possible that Huscroft's cabin was still standing, and if so, it might save me.

The winds were now really picking up, long gray clouds drifting across the bay. The air felt humid, and I knew things were about to get very wet.

If I couldn't find the old cabin, I had no idea what I would do. It was possible it had sunk into the ground long ago.

I pulled myself up and brushed off the sand, amazed at how utterly filthy I was. My clothes were so dirty that they blended into the same brown color as my hands and arms. I had thought that being in the water would clean everything up, but it hadn't seemed to make much difference, other than to leave me chilled and shivering.

Cenotaph, like the rest of the landscape, had been old-growth forest before the tsunami, with the same types of Western hemlock and Sitka spruce that I'd slept under back along the bay.

But this western side of the island was more protected, and here and there giant trees had survived, surrounded by younger trees that had sprung up since the big wave.

I wasn't sure how to find the cabin, but I guessed that Huscroft must have made a path down to the beach to access his boat. If I simply walked along the beach, I might eventually find the path, though the odds were good it was by now completely overgrown.

Reaching the cabin before the storm arrived could be a matter of life and death. Even if it didn't start raining soon, I was going to need drinking water. I had to find that cabin and spring.

I began skirting the forest, and at one point came across a patch of wild asparagus. Even though my stomach still hurt, I stuffed as much as I could inside my shirt, hoping I could eat it later.

I missed my jacket, for not only was it waterproof, but it also kept the cold wind from cutting through me. I wondered if anyone would ever find my driver's license. It didn't seem very likely.

At one point, I saw something pink down on the beach, and thinking it might somehow be berries, walked down to take a look.

But instead of berries, it was a Dungeness crab, one of its claws caught in the rocks. It looked kind of how I felt, forlorn and doomed.

I knew I should kill it and eat it, but the thought made me queasy. I moved the rocks, freeing it, then watched as it scurried away. I felt that somehow this act of kindness helped make up for killing the salmon.

I was exhausted, but had no choice except to continue looking for the cabin. I now had a headache, and a feeling of deep gloom was beginning to replace my earlier optimism.

I felt that my headache was probably caused by the change in pressure, for the wind was now really picking up. Had the kittiwakes taken to their nests on the other side of Cenotaph?

The northern side of the island was only about a third of a mile from where I'd landed on the small spit, and as I walked, I could see where the beach began to curve. I'd now walked the whole western shoreline and hadn't seen anything even vaguely like a path.

I began walking back, looking even harder for a change

in vegetation or any clue that might show me where Huscroft's trail had been.

I was almost back to the small spit when I caught a glimpse of something that looked out of place, something shiny, tangled in the vegetation at the edge of the forest.

It was a beat-up tin cup tangled in what turned out to be a nice patch of huckleberries. The cup had to have been Huscroft's, and the cabin must be nearby, as I knew he'd built it on higher ground above the beach.

I stopped to pick some berries, adding them to the asparagus in my shirt. And it was then that, over the incessant wind, I thought I heard something. I stopped and listened, and it seemed far away, like a long-ago dream, but I recognized it instantly.

It was that same long undulating howl I'd heard earlier!

Instinctively running for the cover of the forest, I slipped into the trees, looking back in the direction from where the sound had come, far up the bay. But I saw nothing through the wind, which was now blowing sand so hard it felt like it was scouring my eyes.

I had to find the cabin, or all would be lost.

9

I was again on super-alert, thinking of the huge tracks I'd found and wondering if the creature would swim the bay to come after me. I somehow knew it would.

Even though I was tired and weak, I tried to hurry, and what I soon found was disheartening. It was the remnants of an old building scattered everywhere, the logs half-rotted into oblivion and covered with moss.

It had to have been Huscroft's cabin, and there was no way it would now offer any shelter to anyone. The logs were too soggy to even use for a fire, even if I'd had some way of starting one.

I turned away and leaned against a huge spruce, bracing myself against the howling wind. The doom had now taken hold of me like a wolf, and I feared it would drag me under until I completely lost what willpower I'd regained.

It was then that I recalled that Huscroft had several outbuildings where he'd stored the big barrels of coho that he harvested and sold to fishermen to help supplement his income.

Once a year, he would hitch a ride with a fishing boat

into Juneau and sell the fish, then resupply himself with goods like flour, tobacco, and matches.

There was no spring nearby, so I decided that this had to have been a storage shed, and the cabin had to be higher up. I again began bushwhacking my way upwards through the thick vegetation.

I was soon next to a small rivulet of water, and I followed it to its source, where an old iron pipe was stuck into the hillside.

I'd found Huscroft's spring, and I drank as much as I could of the cool pure water—the only water on the entire island, according to my research.

I could now make out an old cabin through the thick foliage, and it looked like enough was left of the walls and roof to maybe provide shelter from the incoming storm.

The cabin was guarded by spiky stalks of devil's club, which I carefully brushed through, but I soon found that the door wouldn't budge, as it was sealed by thick vines.

I hesitantly crawled through the only window, and once inside, the single room was musty and smelled of rodents, but was dry.

I was amazed at how stout the walls were. The trees must've been really old to be so large. How had Huscroft managed to stack them alone?

The light inside was dim, but I did make out some empty pints of whiskey littering the floor and an ancient moldy calendar still hung on a nail on the wall, its dates long faded away. Several old matchbooks with faded advertising were strewn on the floor, also covered with mold.

Huscroft had built a fireplace from beach rocks, and a stack of driftwood sat nearby, now green with lichen.

The floor was covered in dead ferns, and I gathered them together to make a soft bed. There, sitting in the ferns,

I slowly ate the wild asparagus I'd stuffed into my shirt, followed by huckleberries, trying to regain my strength.

Leaning back against the wall, I rested and listened to the wind howling outside, thinking of the otherworldly scream I'd heard down at the beach.

It soon started raining, and the wind was now blowing water in through the open window. I knew I needed to somehow seal it off. It would not only make the cabin warmer, but would hopefully make it more secure from bears. I tried not to think about whatever else might be out there.

Carefully wedging pieces of driftwood into the open window, I pounded them in tight with the bottom of the tin cup. The window wasn't completely secure, but it seemed good enough to keep out the rain and any small intruders.

I knew I would now stay dry, and I silently thanked Huscroft for building such a strong cabin.

And as I leaned there against the wall, resting on the soft dead ferns, I realized how exhausted I was.

I needed sleep. If the blue creature I'd heard screaming into the wind would leave me alone, perhaps I could get some rest while the storm blew through, and I might have another chance at things.

10

The Tlingit believe in an earthquake god, and it was the middle of the night when their god, Kah Lituya, woke me.

Kah Lituya means *Man of Lituya*, and he lives deep in an underground cavern near the mouth of the bay.

Kah Lituya gets very angry when someone dares to disturb the bay. He shakes everything, turning the sea into chaos, then changes that person into a bear.

I thought of what the pilot had said about all the bears at Lituya Bay—was this why? I laughed at the thought.

In any case, Kah Lituya must have been angry, for I was awakened by the strangest phenomenon I'd ever experienced—the entire cabin seemed to be oscillating. It seemed almost as if I were inside a giant electrical motor.

I was later told by a geologist that these were the P or primary waves of an earthquake.

P waves travel through the interior of the earth and arrive before surface waves. What I was feeling was seismic energy oscillating through the island.

This oscillation was more puzzling than frightening, and it went on for about 30 seconds before the actual surface wave arrived, which shook the cabin as if a large truck had slammed against it.

My intuition said to get outside, for the cabin's logs would surely crush me, but it was all over before I could do anything, and the cabin still stood, unscathed. I knew it wasn't the first earthquake it had seen.

Later, I found out the quake had registered a 5.8. This is considered moderate, but I was sure that some of the steep mountains surrounding the bay had experienced landslides.

If I'd been outside, I might have heard the rumbling, but who knows, the wind was roaring so hard, it would've been hard to hear anything.

I wondered if this was a foreshock and if something bigger was on the way. Even though I was weak and exhausted, I couldn't sleep.

And as the night wore on, another wave seemed to oscillate over me—a wave of foreboding, all mixed with vibrating earthquake waves, giant footprints, something blue-gray lurking back in the forest shadows, and a terrifying howl.

I wasn't sure if I were awake or dreaming, and I later decided I must be having hallucinations. I finally slipped into a deep sleep, but not for long, as something else woke me.

I could immediately tell that something was different, but I couldn't figure out what it was.

It then dawned on me that the wind had died down, and the sun was coming up, for I could now see inside the cabin. It was still raining, and I again slipped into a dreamless sleep.

When I awoke, I felt somewhat rested, but I knew I had to find more food soon, as I was getting weaker and weaker.

My body wasn't used to eating raw fish and berries, and my stomach hurt.

I pulled the driftwood from the window and looked outside. Everything was dripping, and water had pooled near the front door, but I was dry, and the rain had stopped. I could see an orange tint in the east and knew the sun was rising.

Slipping back out the window, I used my tin cup to drink from the spring, then made my way through the thick vegetation down to the beach.

What a sight! Kah Lituya must have decided I was welcome after all, as he'd prepared a feast for me.

The beach was littered with thousands of shrimp, as well as scallops and an occasional crab. Salmon and halibut lay everywhere, some still slapping and gasping in the air.

It appeared that the earthquake had somehow dredged sea life up from the bay, as shrimp are deep-water creatures. There must have been a tsunami, and I was glad the cabin sat on higher ground.

I immediately set about throwing fish that were still alive back into the water, although many had already died. I then sat on a rock and feasted on raw shrimp, wishing I could somehow cook them, as well as the fish and scallops.

Finally, when I could hold no more, I took off my shirt and wrapped as many fish, shrimp, and scallops in it as it would hold, then started back to the cabin, wishing there was some way I could cook or dry the meat.

Back at the cabin, I spread the bounty out on the fireplace, then spent some time arranging the dead ferns into a better bed while my shirt dried.

The cabin now smelled like a wharf, and I hoped some bear didn't mistake the cabin for a storehouse and break in.

I spent the rest of the day gathering berries and drinking

from the spring and resting. I was feeling much better, also realizing how dehydrated I'd become.

It seemed as if my body was beginning to acclimate somewhat to eating raw food, as my stomach no longer ached, and I felt more energetic.

I'd eaten more shrimp and was nestled down into the dried ferns long before dusk, the driftwood again crammed into the window.

As I tried to sleep, a fierce wind again came up, but this time from the direction opposite the Gulf of Alaska.

I knew this was a katabatic wind, a downslope wind coming off the snow-clad peaks of the Fairweather Range, a wind created when the mountain surface is colder than the surrounding air.

The storm that had come in off the Gulf of Alaska had moved on through, replaced by this high front.

I'd read one account by a native who'd said that in the winter, ferocious katabatic winds often came screaming down the peaks at over 100 m.p.h., turning the water into complete chaos. Sometimes it would generate waves that went completely over the top of Cenotaph Island.

And as I lay there, I again thought of the blue-gray creature and wondered if it knew where I was.

The ominous feeling I'd had earlier had passed, and I soon fell asleep, dreaming I was hiking across a green field in Utah, Max at my heels.

But my happy place was soon to disappear.

11

Someone was tapping on the driftwood that sealed the window, and when it woke me, I could tell it was dawn.

I quietly got up, wondering if it wasn't some kind of bird, as the tapping was rhythmic and subdued.

I slipped over near the window, not wanting whatever it was to know I was there, yet wanting to be ready in case it was a bear or something worse. I didn't know what I could do, but being alert surely couldn't hurt.

Had it smelled all the fish and shrimp inside?

I heard a deep gravelly voice. "Let me in. I need help."

I couldn't process what I was hearing. Surely it had to be the wind playing tricks, though it seemed to have died down.

"Please. Let me in. I need help."

"Who are you?" I asked.

"I've been wrecked on the spit. I'm the only one who made it. Please…"

I pulled the driftwood from the window, and a shaggy-haired man climbed in, wet and shivering. He was stocky and muscular and looked like he could have easily broken in if he'd wanted.

He tumbled onto the floor, where he rocked back and forth on his haunches.

"What happened?" I asked, tense and wondering how I could possibly help this man.

He looked up, and I could barely make out his bloodshot eyes. He said, "I was in the wheelhouse. I held my brother's hand as we went down. I never saw him or the others again."

I stood in shock. Apparently another boat had gone down at the entrance to Lituya Bay. What had they been doing trying to enter in the storm? It would have been suicidal.

"I was on the *Arctic Shadow*, a crab boat. I told the captain we needed to avoid the bay and stay out to sea, but he said the boat was going to roll in the high waves. We'd loaded too many crab pots on it and were overweight. We'd already almost rolled twice in the wind. He said we had to get into the bay."

The man shook his head as if he couldn't believe his own tale, then continued. "We got crosswise at the entrance just as a big surge came from the bay, and the boat rolled onto the rocks. It only took minutes to sink. I tried to operate the hydraulic system for the lifeboat, but it was stuck. Most of the crew were below in their bunks, sleeping. They never had a chance."

He began sobbing, then composed himself, and eyeing the old bottles, asked, "Do you have any whiskey? I could use some. But there's not enough alcohol in the world that could ever drown these memories. I managed to swim to shore, then found tracks that came up here."

He began rocking again, asking, "What the hell happened?"

"There was an earthquake," I replied. "It must have caused the surge that made the boat roll."

I felt terrible for this man, losing his brother and ship-mates, but I felt even more concerned for his future here—who knew if he could survive? I wasn't even sure I could.

And yet, it would be good to have company, someone who could perhaps help figure out an escape. And maybe two people would be more intimidating to bears—as well as to the blue creature.

He now said softly, his chest heaving, "I can hear the screams of the crew. It will haunt me forever."

"How could you hear them scream if they were all in the hold?" I asked. "All but your brother, I mean."

As soon as I'd asked it, my question seemed insensitive, and I wished I could take it back.

The man answered, now talking rapidly, "I saw their final moments, even though they were in the boat. It was horrible. We'd been in 60 m.p.h. winds and 20-foot seas. We had to find anchor somewhere. We knew we were near Lituya Bay."

He paused, then added, "It's a notorious stretch of water, not only because of the wind, but from the strong currents, and the entrance is too shallow. It has the reputation of being a real hell hole. When you come up to the spit, it sucks you in, and you'd better be straight on. The current there stands the seas straight up, sharp as a knife until they break. And now everyone's gone."

I was sorry for the man but confused. Something wasn't right. How could he have seen his crew's final moments when they were in the hold and he was on deck?

The man seemed to sense my confusion and said, "When I drift off to sleep it happens again and again. The water pours in, and the crew fights for their lives. I'm the only one who survived. I wasn't rescued for a week, and I was hunted the entire time by a blue-gray monster. Nobody believes me."

The man now let out a wail, and I worried the blue creature would hear him. But he then disappeared, his face lingering for a moment with a look of angst.

I now realized I was dreaming, but instead of waking, the dream changed, and I was in a large church where everyone was crying.

An older woman dressed in black stood and sobbed, "Why did all these good men go down at sea?"

Another woman, younger and wearing a gray dress, said, "I've lived in Alaska my whole life. Fishing is a great life until the day they don't come home. You never know what happened."

The man who'd been talking to me moments before was also there, but now wearing a black suit, his hair and beard neatly trimmed.

He sat in the back, and without rising, said, "The pain will never go away. Even though these men are gone, their memory will live on forever."

I finally woke, feeling like I'd just climbed Mount Fairweather. There was no one in the cabin with me, and the window was still boarded up. Light now shone through the cracks in the driftwood.

I felt a chill come over me as I recalled reading about the *Arctic Shadow* some time ago. It had gone down the autumn before in the mouth of Lituya Bay. There had been only one survivor, and he'd later taken his own life, possibly because of survivor's guilt.

Had I seen a ghost? I found it hard to believe, as I'd never really believed in spirits or the supernatural. It had to have been a dream, even though I thought I could smell a faint hint of diesel fuel, the same smell one might have on their work clothes after operating a lifeboat engine.

The sense of foreboding was back, now stronger than ever.

12

I continued to sleep in the cabin, and each day I began to feel more and more at home. I got myself into a routine where I would search for something to eat, sometimes in the nearby forest, and sometimes down on the beach.

When I did go down to the beach, I was always careful to stay as hidden as possible and stay on rocks, not walking on the sand unless I had to. I didn't want to leave any tracks.

I'd eaten well for awhile, but after a few days, the shrimp were mostly gone, and what was left was rotting away. The feast had also been enjoyed by the seabirds and otters and such.

In the meantime, I'd found several berry stands, as well as more asparagus and parsley and a nice patch of chanterelle mushrooms.

I was getting used to not being able to cook anything, and even though I knew I was gaunt and thin, I was starting to feel better.

In addition, my desultory attitude had improved, and I hoped I could survive long enough to somehow signal a fishing boat if one ever entered the bay.

Sometimes I would go sit on Passage Rock, directly across from the terminus of La Chaussee Spit, watching for boats. I was sure to be seen there, but I never did see anyone come in.

It became a habit to go to the rock and watch every afternoon far into the evening, wishing I were on the occasional float plane that always flew too high above to see me.

I watched the birds and wildlife carefully, and if I saw them eating something, I figured it would also be safe for me to eat.

I discovered many edible plants that way, and except for an occasional salmon, which I was now more adept at dispatching somewhat painlessly, I knew to stay away from anything that was red.

I had pretty much completely forgotten that I'd come to Lituya Bay to die, and in some ways my life had never seemed fuller. The only thing that bothered me much— except Max and the fact that winter was coming—was the thought of the blue creature.

I'd completely lost track of how long I'd been on Cenotaph Island, but it may have been about my third week there when I had another strange dream.

The Tlingit, masters of water and boating, believe that drowning is the worst possible way to die, especially if the body is lost. They believe that the soul is reincarnated into another person, with cremation being a necessary part of this transformation.

Those whose bodies are lost to water can't be reincarnated and instead became dangerous creatures called kooshdakhaaa, or kushtaka, which translates into *land-otter man*—beings doomed to a netherworld between the living and dead.

Land-otter men have the bodies of a human, but are

covered with hair and have a tail like an otter. They're dangerous and can appear or disappear without warning, as well as look and talk like people you know.

It's considered a very bad thing to see or talk to one, for their main purpose is to lure you to your death so you can become one of them.

I'd forgotten reading about them until the night my ex-wife came into the cabin and stood over me, crying, begging me to come home, sorry for all that had happened.

It was so real that I stood up, wanting to hold her, but she disappeared. I was sure I hadn't been dreaming, and it left me feeling panicked and scared. Had I just seen a kushtaka?

It took several days for me to regain my equilibrium after that, and I kept having the feeling that I was being watched, just like I'd felt when sleeping in the forest duff after I'd first arrived.

Now the unsettling dreams began coming more and more often. I dreamt of the many explorers who had been killed entering the bay—the Russians, the French, and the many gold miners, as well as various natives and non-native fishermen.

Most often, I would dream I was sitting across from the spit watching a boat come in. It would lose control, start listing, then be crumpled against the rocks.

I could always hear the sounds of the dying, and then I'd see what looked like ghosts walking up and down the spit.

Were they land-otter men? I would wake, sweating and disoriented, not sure where I was.

I finally got to where I dreaded going to sleep each night, and this led to me becoming sleep deprived, which probably led to even more strange dreams.

But the one thing that became an almost daily occurrence was the horrible howl wafting across the waters from up the bay.

I hoped that the blue creature hadn't realized where I'd gone, and it seemed like my hope was well-founded so far, as it always sounded angry, but distant.

It gave me a chill and made me vow to somehow get away from the bay.

Maybe I could take a log from Huscroft's storage building and make my way back across the bay to the south, then begin walking the coastline to Glacier Bay.

Or perhaps I should go the other direction, walking towards the Tlingit village of Yakutat, the only permanent community along the outer coast.

But I knew either direction would be extremely difficult, and my odds of running into bears or getting blocked by cliffs were good. Plus, I would be exposed to any storm that came off the gulf, without having even a jacket.

My clothes were already in tatters, and the soles of my shoes were about to come off, the glue disintegrating from always being wet. I knew I couldn't leave the shelter the cabin provided. It seemed as if I was stuck.

I began spending more and more time out on the point, watching, hoping someone would come.

One afternoon, as I sat there, the earth again began to shake—it was another earthquake. This was much smaller than the first one, but I again had a foreboding that what I was experiencing was another foreshock, and a bigger quake was coming.

I'd noticed that the kittiwakes and gulls had been flightier than usual that morning, making more keening noises and flying in huge arcs above the bay, disturbed by something.

Somehow, they'd known the earthquake was coming. I vowed to watch them more closely in the future.

This earthquake was smaller than the 5.8 I'd felt before, but I could still hear the sound of rocks falling across the bay. I was grateful that I was up several hundred feet above the water.

I sat up there for a long time, but I never saw anything like a tsunami or even a large wave.

But it was that same day, still sitting on the point, that I saw something walking along the spit.

I instinctively drew back into the forest where I could watch and not be seen.

It looked exactly like a land-otter man, tall and thin, with an otter's tail dragging behind. I wasn't able to see its face, but it left me with a feeling of hopelessness.

It wasn't a half hour later that I heard the cry of the blue creature, and a chill came over me, for it was now much closer. It sounded like it was coming down the beach towards Cenotaph Island.

The land-otter man seemed to disappear into thin air, and I stood there wondering if I hadn't finally completely lost my mind.

13

The next night, I had yet another dream, one that left me frightened and vowing that I would somehow leave the next day, even if I had to swim off the island and start walking.

The day of that dream, I'd gone down to the beach, hoping to find a fish or something to eat. It had been several days since I'd had any kind of protein, and my stomach again felt like a hard knot.

I'd been eating nothing but berries and asparagus for the previous few days. Since arriving, I'd been scouring the forest all around the cabin, finding cloudberries, raspberries, and salmon berries, but it now looked as if I'd depleted the area.

I needed to expand my range, but I hated going down to the beach, as I always felt exposed.

Once down there, I always felt that same sense of foreboding and wondered if the blue creature might be nearby.

But I finally had no choice if I wanted to eat, so I walked down the hill from the cabin.

I thought again of the land-otter man I'd seen the

previous day walking out on the spit, and I knew I needed to be very careful.

Once at the beach, I soon found another set of tracks. I felt nauseous and immediately headed back up to the cabin, a sense of doom accompanying me.

The creature had finally come to Cenotaph.

It was shortly thereafter that I again heard the howl, but this time it sounded very close, so close that the undulating sound waves felt like a punch to my stomach.

It sounded like it was right below the cabin, and I wondered if it would find the path up there. I knew it had to be a matter of time.

There would be no going to Passage Rock that day to watch for boats, I thought as I crammed the wood back into the windows as tightly as possible, knowing full well it would never stop the creature.

Now what? It was a beautiful day, but I was afraid to go outside, and I had nothing to eat. I'd filled the old cup with water earlier, setting it on the fireplace, and that would have to last until I was thirsty enough that I had no choice but to go outside.

I hunkered down in the dry ferns, which were becoming flatter each day, and took stock of where I was.

I'd come to the bay only a few weeks earlier to die, but I'd never guessed that I might die by the hands of some strange creature that I'd never even known existed. I was sure it would be a violent and gruesome death, probably even worse than death by bear.

And come to think of it, where were the bears? I'd seen neither hide nor hair of any since finding the tracks when I'd first arrived.

The area was supposed to be full of them, and they

could easily swim to the island. Were they also afraid of the creature? Had they all fled?

Was the creature simply staking out its territory and trying to scare me away? I didn't want to know, for all I cared about was going home.

But I had no home to go to. At this point, I had no home, no possessions, no family. My clothes were almost gone, and I didn't even have an ID. I'd become Nemo, nobody.

It then dawned on me that I also had no responsibilities. I'd become totally and completely free since coming to the island, eventually letting go of most of my negative memories.

No one knew where I was, and I realized that I kind of liked it that way. My kids were fine without me, and the only one I really missed was Max. If I could only get Max back, my life would be complete.

I laughed, thinking how foolish most people would think that statement sounded.

My life would be complete, even though I had nothing, my stomach hurt, and I was holed up in an old cabin in the Alaskan wilderness, afraid for my life, slowly starving to death. I'd read that people feel more alive when threatened with dying, so I must be *really* alive, I mused.

As I lay there, curled up in the dead ferns, I suddenly became aware of a musky odor, something that reminded me of the smell of mink or weasels. I wondered if it weren't the blue creature, though it smelled different from the musky smell before.

Now it seemed as if someone were standing in the far corner of the cabin, someone not much more than an ethereal shadow, tall and thin and covered in brown fur. It had a long pointed nose and dark liquid eyes.

Could it be a land-otter man? If so, how did it get in here? The driftwood was still sealed tight.

I tried not to move. Maybe it wouldn't see me in the shadows. I had to be hallucinating. My energy reserves were getting low. I needed food.

It now spoke in an ominous yet somewhat squeaky voice, saying, "I asked Kah Lituya to make you one of us. He at first said no, that you deserved to live, but we argued until he gave in."

It stopped speaking until I thought it must be finished, but then continued.

"Tomorrow, you will try to escape, but instead of leaving, you will join us. By this time tomorrow night, there will be three new kushtaka—including you and the blue one. We've wanted the blue one for a long time, but until today, he would never swim. We almost got him today, but he unfortunately made it to shore."

I remembered the tracks I'd seen on the beach this morning. I'd been right! The blue creature had indeed made it to the island.

The land-otter man stood in silence as if sizing me up, then added, "Tomorrow, if the blue one seeks your help, deny him. If you don't, Kah Lituya will be very angry and will destroy everything, and you will be responsible. You will then suffer greatly when you become a kushtaka."

I knew I had to be hallucinating. The blue one would need my help? The creature that wanted me dead? How could it possibly need my help?

I sighed. Was this whole thing just a dream? Was I somehow in a coma in a hospital? The only way I could explain all this was through outright insanity or some kind of medical problem. It couldn't possibly be real.

"How can you possibly be real?" I asked, but the land-otter man was gone, the smell of musk fading.

I thought about what it had said. If this weren't a dream and was real, the land-otter man had told me I would die tomorrow, so didn't that mean that today I could do whatever I wanted with impunity? Maybe today would be a good day to escape.

I laughed at the logic, or lack of it, removed the drift-wood from the window, and stepped out into the damp forest, wondering if the blue creature was nearby.

It then occurred to me that the land-otter man had said there would be three new kushtaka tomorrow.

Who was the third?

14

I spent the rest of the day looking for food, though the only thing I could find was more asparagus.

Drinking from the spring, I wondered if this might actually be my last day alive. I again thought of my jacket and ID, wondering if anyone would ever find it.

I began wondering what it would feel like to be a land-otter man. What did they do all day, just wander around looking for people they could scare? Or did they hang out with Kah Lituya, begging him to destroy things?

It didn't sound like a particularly boring existence, and maybe I would actually enjoy it. They had to be good swimmers, if spirits could swim.

I tried laughing it all off, saying I wasn't superstitious, but the entire time I was looking for something to eat, I had the feeling I was being watched. Several times, I turned quickly to look, but never saw anything.

Both the land-otter man and the sight of the tracks confirmed what I'd suspected, that the blue creature was now on the island.

Of course, I was assuming the land-otter man was real, and it was more likely it was a figment of my starving brain.

At one point, I thought I could hear something large walking nearby through the undergrowth, but the vegetation was too thick to see very far. I hid until I thought it was gone.

Finally, feeling tired and threatened, I filled my tin cup with water and crawled back through the cabin window.

It was only late afternoon, but all I wanted to do was sleep, my energy depleted. I was once again feeling that I would never leave the island alive, and my vision of the land-otter man had left me depressed.

I boarded up the window and again curled up. It seemed that even though I fell asleep easily, I never felt rested when I woke. I didn't want to go to sleep because of the strange dreams, but I also recognized that they were most likely from being malnourished.

One's brain begins to do strange things when it's starved for glucose, its main source of energy. In fact, after the body's reserves are depleted, there's evidence that the brain starts to metabolize its own neurons.

I hadn't had much extra fat on me when I'd arrived at the bay, and I knew that while here I'd been depleting my body's stores of vitamins and minerals, as well as muscle.

Was I now burning brain tissue for energy? Was this the real source of the land-otter man and the blue creature and my lack of cognitive clarity?

It was possible that I'd never actually read about land-otter men and had conjured it all up, but I knew the blue creature was real. The terror I'd felt as it stood over me had been undeniable, and I'd actually seen it in the distance, long before I'd become malnourished.

I must've fallen asleep, for it was much later that something woke me. Something was different, but it took me a few minutes to figure out what it was.

Pink light filtered in through the driftwood at the window, and I knew there had to be a fire.

I quickly pulled off the wood and crawled outside. If the forest was burning, I needed to flee.

What I saw took my breath away. The evening sky was a vibrant pink-orange, soon turning a luminous, intensely bright shade of reddish-pink. I'd never seen anything like it, and it seemed surreal, almost like the end of the world.

But even stranger was the sight of thousands of birds wheeling through the sky, obviously disturbed by something.

Some species I could identify, and some I'd never seen before. There were of course the kittiwakes and gulls and ravens, but I also saw grebes, sandhill cranes, Canada geese, mallards, and even what looked to be swans. A lone albatross winged silently over me, looking lost.

The brilliant reddish-pink sky seemed to last forever, and I finally crawled back through the window, sealing it back up.

I felt that something was about to change, but I wasn't sure what. Like the birds circling above, I had a sense of unrest, of wanting to flee. I suddenly wanted to go down to the beach, as the cabin now felt claustrophobic instead of sheltering.

Was there an earthquake coming? Did the birds know something I didn't know? If there was a tsunami, the beach would not be a good place to be. I should instead climb to the highest point on the island, but I was afraid of what I might encounter out there.

I decided to stay in the cabin and try to rest until morning, then I would go again to Passage Rock and hope for rescue.

Later, when I got back to civilization, my geologist friend Doug told me that what I'd seen was called an "earthquake sky."

It was considered by many to be the harbinger of a major quake, though there was no real scientific evidence for such.

He himself had talked to a man who'd seen an earthquake sky before the 7.2 Hebgen Quake in southern Montana near the town of West Yellowstone. That quake had caused a massive landslide that killed 28 people.

The man had been a kid at the time, and he and a friend were walking home from a baseball game. They saw an older guy waving them over to his front porch.

The sky was intense red, the clouds rapidly moving, and the old man told them there would be an earthquake soon and to prepare themselves. The Hebgen Quake struck that night.

When I asked Doug what could possibly cause an earthquake sky, he said he didn't know, but maybe it had something to do with the fact that most rock has grains of quartz, and quartz has electrical properties when under pressure.

Whatever caused it, I would soon learn that the bright sky was indeed a harbinger of destruction, and Kah Lituya was definitely angry.

15

I felt as if my life had become a fog, a continuum of restless sleep surrounding strange dreams followed by even stranger days awake. But the next 24 hours would surpass anything I'd known, and in retrospect, it was the most intense and inexplicable day of my life.

I awoke sometime in the dark, and I'd again had a strange dream, one that made all the others seem mild.

I shivered, for I could still see the horrible image, even though I had my eyes open.

It was the blue creature, and it was standing above me. It had the ugliest face I'd ever seen, with a heavy brow and deep-set black eyes, and it appeared to be grinning, its wide lips pulled back and its blocky yellow teeth visible.

In spite of its ugliness, I found it to be strangely attractive, for its fur was the most beautiful satiny silver-blue I'd ever seen. I wanted to reach out and stroke it, and yet I was terrified.

I closed my eyes and opened them again. There was nothing there. I'd again been hallucinating.

That was followed by yet another dream. I was in a small

boat, more like a kayak or canoe, and someone behind me was paddling.

We were in great danger, and we had very little time to escape something terrible and threatening. It seemed it could be a tsunami, but I wasn't sure—all I knew was that there was a feeling of urgency.

Now the boat was skimming along faster and faster, and I turned to see large chunks of ice overcoming us as the water rose. I yelled to the rower, but the wind took the words from my mouth.

We were soon overcome by several large chunks of ice, one of which banged against the canoe, nearly capsizing us. It bumped up against where I sat, and as I looked down, I could see it was only maybe six inches thick, and I remember thinking it would be easy to smash, if only I had a paddle.

But the boatman wouldn't give me his, which made me angry, as I knew the ice would tip us over if I didn't act quickly. We would become land-otter men.

But now I could see something under the ice, something almost the same color, but with hints of blue-gray.

As the ice slammed harder against the canoe, I realized the blue-gray thing was the face of the blue creature, its dark eyes looking up through the ice in terror.

Somehow it had been caught under ice from the glaciers and was now stuck, the tsunami carrying it out to sea. I knew it would soon be dead if I did nothing.

It was then that I recalled the words of the land-otter man: "If the blue one seeks your help, deny him. If you don't, Kah Lituya will be very angry and will destroy everything, and you will be responsible. You will then suffer greatly when you become a kushtaka."

I pulled back, looking away. As far as I knew, this creature had been hunting me, terrorizing me with its howls, and it had spared me so far only because it hadn't been able to find me.

Why should I do anything to help it? How many others had it killed? And the odds were good that if I saved it, it would come back and kill me anyway.

I pushed against the big chunk of ice with my hands, and it caught a wave and floated away in another direction, creature and all.

Now fully awake, I remembered where I was and tried to center myself. I was sweating and shaking, but I soon was able to see Max's face in my mind's eye instead of the creature.

I tried to go to my happy place, but instead I saw Max in the back yard of what had once been my house, looking thin and unkempt, waiting for me to return.

How long had I been gone? Why had I been so ineffective at getting away from Lituya Bay? Even though I'd felt a sense of competence after surviving for awhile, this feeling was slowly being replaced by one of lassitude and hopelessness.

Maybe I was meant to die here and should just accept that fact and get on with it.

I could now see faint light filtering through the gaps in the cabin window, and I knew it was nearly dawn. There hadn't been an earthquake yet, so maybe the colored sky had a different explanation.

In any case, I needed to leave the cabin and figure out some way to escape Cenotaph and the bay. I had to prove the land-otter man wrong. I had to escape and get Max.

I stood and brushed myself off, then grabbed my tin cup, realizing that I did still own something.

After I returned to civilization, I would keep that cup as

a reminder of my own strengths, as well as a reminder of how we need others. But at that time, I knew getting away was beyond me. I needed someone to help.

As I removed the driftwood from the window, I was shocked to see a face looking in at me.

At first I thought it was a kushtaka, but I soon knew that instead, my wish had been granted.

But my hope of escape was soon overcome by the realization that this had to be the third person destined to become a land-otter man.

16

"You have to come with me quickly now," said the small lithe man who I took to be Tlingit. "We don't have much time."

He grabbed my arm and pulled me through the window.

I was weak, too weak to argue, and to tell the truth, I wasn't even sure he was real.

We hurried down the path, him half dragging me, much stronger than his small size would suggest.

He wore a blue t-shirt with red letters that read, "YU Rec," and I guessed he must be from Yakutat, the nearest Tlingit village, on up the coast to the north.

I was panting and puffing, having trouble keeping up with him, and I finally asked him to stop for a moment so I could catch my breath.

"Where are we going?" I asked, not really caring very much.

"My family was across the bay on our annual berry-picking trip here," he replied. "We usually spend a week, but after only a few hours, my grandfather said there was something wrong. It was then that we heard the blue one. It's not been seen here for many years, as it usually stays far up on the glaciers below Fairweather."

We hurried down the path towards the beach as he continued. "We decided to leave, and on the way out of the bay, my uncle saw you for a moment. We thought at first you were a..." he paused, so I finished the sentence for him.

"A land-otter man?" I asked.

He looked surprised. "Yes, a kushtaka."

"I may become one soon," I replied, still not sure if he was real.

"Don't speak of them," he replied. "Hurry."

We were now at the edge of the forest, and the man paused, looking carefully both directions before helping me down to the beach where a small two-person kayak was tied to a rock.

I crawled into the front of the boat, then he pushed it away from the shore and jumped in behind me, picking up the paddle.

We were soon away from shore, heading out and around the small cove I'd landed on when I'd come to Cenotaph.

"It's good to be on the water," he said, looking relieved. "The blue one is on Cenotaph, and I was worried it would push the kayak out to sea. We can't go through the entrance, as it's hours until slack tide. We'll cross over to the spit and portage. I'm Dennis Skookum. Who are you?"

"Nemo," I replied.

He studied me for a moment, perplexed, then asked, "Nemo? Like the guy in the Jules Verne story? Latin for *nobody*?"

I replied, "I think my name is really Joe, but it's been a long time. But why are you helping me?"

"Well, you look like you need it," Dennis answered. "How long has it been since you had something to eat?"

I shrugged my shoulders.

"There's food on the boat," he replied.

"The boat?"

"My family's on our salmon boat, waiting along the coastline. My grandfather anchored it out of the bay. But I decided to come back for you in one of our kayaks."

"Thank you," I said quietly, the reality of my rescue beginning to sink in.

"You're welcome," Dennis replied. "But it isn't just for you. My grandfather says that Kah Lituya is angry because you're on the island. We wanted to get you out before he becomes so angry he destroys everything, like he's done before."

Dennis was now paddling hard towards the spit, and I wondered why he'd decided to portage across instead of waiting until the entrance was passable.

"When is slack high tide?" I asked.

He replied, "We can't wait. We need to portage. I'm taking us to a spot where there's not much vegetation. We need to get out of the bay as soon as possible."

I thought he must be afraid the blue creature would somehow follow us, so I said, "The land-otter man told me the blue thing can't swim very well. I don't think it will come after us."

Dennis stopped rowing. "You talked to a kushtaka?"

I knew I'd screwed up somehow, that what I'd done was probably taboo, so I just shrugged my shoulders and said, "I've been delirious."

Dennis said nothing more, and we were soon at the spit, where he steered the kayak towards a break in the foliage. He soon jumped out and dragged the boat to shore, then helped me out.

"Do you think you have enough strength to help carry this thing?" he asked. "It's not that heavy."

"I'll do my best," I said as he hoisted the front of the kayak onto his shoulders. I grabbed the rear and tried to help, and even though it was surprisingly light, he ended up doing most of the work. Fortunately, the spit wasn't far across, only a few hundred feet, but it was rocky.

As we carried on, I realized that the blue creature must not be all that poor of a swimmer after all, for I could hear it screaming, and it sounded like it wasn't far away, following us.

"Hurry!" Dennis commanded. "It's coming across."

I stumbled along behind him until a stiff wind hit, nearly knocking me down. We'd crossed the spit and were now on one of the most rugged shores in North America, the southeast Alaska coast, now directly on the Gulf of Alaska, with nothing to buffer us from its fierce weather.

Big waves broke against the shore, and I wondered how Dennis intended to push off to sea.

I could see what looked like a small salmon boat anchored a good half-mile off the shore, back away from the beach where the water was calm, and I assumed it was his family.

Looking back towards the end of the spit, I could see crescent-shaped waves entering the bay, and I knew these were the same waves that had spun numerous boats into the rocks, making land-otter men of their crews.

Suddenly, the creature screamed, and it seemed to be much closer.

Without hesitation, Dennis dragged the kayak down to the shore, motioned for me to jump in, and was soon behind me, his paddles gracefully pushing through the waves. I knew I was seeing a skill that had been handed down through many generations of Tlingit.

Just as we crested the waves and got to calmer water, we could hear a loud roaring behind us. At first, I thought it was the creature, but I then realized it was coming from way up the bay, up towards the glaciers. Dennis began paddling even harder towards the salmon boat.

I now thought of how the land-otter man had predicted this would be the day that I and the blue creature would die, along with one other. That one other had to be Dennis. I felt like time had stopped.

Looking back, I saw a tidal wave, a tsunami, crest over the spit and come out to sea, close behind us, carrying logs and big chunks of ice. Would it push the kayak under and drown Dennis and I? I didn't want to be a land-otter man, a kushtaka, I wanted to go get Max.

The tsunami soon hit hard, nearly capsizing the kayak, but Dennis skillfully rode it out. The kayak nearly rolled several times, and I knew if it did I wouldn't have the strength to swim.

Dennis later said the wave wasn't really that big when it got to us, maybe only 15 feet, as the spit had slowed it down. To me, it seemed more like a hundred.

I found out later that the earthquake had hit right on the Fairweather Fault, right under the tail of the fish at the end of the bay where the glaciers sat. Because we were out to sea, we never felt the actual quake and dealt only with the tidal wave.

Ecstatic that we were now out of danger, I wasn't ready for the large chunk of ice now headed towards us.

When it dawned on me what it was, I remembered my dream and instantly knew what was beneath it.

17

"If the blue one seeks your help, deny him. If you don't, Kah Lituya will be very angry and will destroy everything, and you will be responsible. You will then suffer greatly when you become a kushtaka."

The words of the land-otter man echoed over and over in my mind as I watched the chunk of ice float dangerously close to the kayak.

One good bump would capsize us, and odds were good Dennis and I would become land-otter men, even though the wave had passed and I'd thought we were out of danger.

Dennis, as deft a kayaker as he was, couldn't seem to push away from the ice, and I knew it was because we were riding the same wave.

But I knew he had no idea what was beneath it, and to be honest, I wasn't entirely sure either. After all, I'd been delirious, and the visit from the land-otter man was surely just a dream.

It would be truly ironic if the premonition, whether a dream or not, came true, and we both became dreaded and feared kushtaka.

Or would I just simply drown and go wherever white men go since I wasn't a Tlingit?

No, I'd dreamt of the others, the Russians, the French, all those lost in the bay, and they'd become land-otter men. Most of them hadn't been Tlingits. Kah Lituya apparently made no distinction, turning everyone into kushtaka.

Now the ice slammed against the boat, and I clenched my teeth, knowing what was coming. The blue creature would be underneath it, its head caught in what looked to be a small air pocket, trying desperately to free itself, an impossible task.

It would look up at me with pleading eyes, and I would turn away, deny it, even though it seemed like Kah Lituya was already destroying everything.

Sure enough, I could now see a blue-gray form beneath the ice, and I felt nauseous as the ice floated alongside the boat, revealing the face I'd dreamed about.

It was exactly like my dream, and I wasn't entirely sure I wasn't dreaming now. Maybe what I'd thought was a dream had been real, and this was the dream.

Through the ice I could make out a huge head, all covered with silver-blue fur surrounding a face that looked to be the blend of an ape and a bear, except it had a flat nose instead of a snout.

I wanted to say it was a Bigfoot, but it looked slightly different from the descriptions of those in the Pacific Northwest.

Who knows, maybe it had descended from Bigfoot but evolved into something else, or maybe it was what the northern First Nations people call the Windigo. The color of its fur certainly indicated it had adapted to the glaciers, much like a glacier bear.

In any case, like in my dream, I thought it was the ugliest

face I'd ever seen. I knew Dennis, who was behind me, had to be able to see the creature, and as I turned and looked back, the fear on his face confirmed my suspicion.

The wave was now flattening, as we were far enough out to sea that the tsunami's energy was becoming submerged.

Without thinking, I reached back and took Dennis's paddle, nodding towards the giant beneath the ice.

He knew what I was going to do, but unlike in the dream, he made no effort to stop me. He seemed to agree that it would be a good thing.

I tried to pry the ice upwards with the paddle, bracing it against the edge of the kayak, but that nearly tipped the boat over.

The creature seemed aware, watching from the small air pocket under the ice, knowing its fate was in my hands.

I could see it trying to push itself down so it could swim free, but each time the ice would rebound, and it had nothing to brace against.

The ice was now starting to float away from the kayak, and I knew I had to act quickly. I took the paddle and slammed it over and over into the ice, trying to not hit the creature. I had to be careful to not break the paddle, leaving us at the mercy of the waves.

With each blow, the creature winced, but I was finally able to break through so it could swim free. It came to the surface, gasping, and I was amazed at how much air it seemed to take into its huge lungs.

It was only a few feet from the kayak, and I wondered if it would grab the boat and pull us under, trying to save itself.

I quickly gave the paddle to Dennis, and he deftly and swiftly moved us from the creature's reach.

We were now several hundred yards from shore, and,

recalling what the land-otter man had said about the creature's swimming abilities, I wondered if I hadn't saved it only to watch it drown.

The creature started to swim for shore, making its way through the waves, as we in turn made our way to the salmon boat.

And as we climbed on board and Dennis's uncle pulled the kayak to the deck, I could see the creature crawl onto the beach far behind us, and I knew it had made it.

I know it sounds odd, but I silently thanked it for restoring my will to live, for freeing me from despair.

Once on the salmon boat, I was too weak to balance myself against the sea's motion, and Dennis quickly helped me below deck where his family waited—his grandparents, his wife and three kids, and his uncle's wife. Dennis's uncle was now in the wheelhouse, steering the boat, having raised the anchor.

They all looked shocked to see the condition I was in, but it wasn't long before someone wrapped a warm blanket around me and brought me a big bowl of hot soup.

After I ate, they took me to a bunk and wrapped more blankets around me. There, in the hold of Dennis's family's boat, I slept a deep sleep unlike any I'd had since first going to Lituya Bay.

Finally, after what must've been hours, Dennis woke me, saying, "We're almost in Yakutat. Are you OK?"

"I think so," I said. "But I've been wondering, why didn't you stop me from freeing the creature?"

He answered thoughtfully, "We Tlingit believe that all life is of equal value—plants, trees, birds, animals, and humans. All are equally respected. Even the ugly."

I nodded and thanked him again for rescuing me. I had no idea what had happened back at the bay, but after finding out it was a 6.2 earthquake, I knew that it was easily big enough to destroy Huscroft's cabin. Given the state I was in, even if I had survived the quake, I would have soon died of exposure.

I next asked Dennis how soon I could get back to Anchorage. I told him I had no money, but I needed to get my dog.

"I'm an EMT for the tribe," Dennis said. "And it looks to me like you're going to need to stay in Yakutat for a few days to recover. When you're better, we can wrangle up some clothes, and then I'm sure you can hitch a plane ride with someone back to Anchorage. In the meantime, I'd like to know more about your time at the bay."

"Thank you," I replied. "I'll be glad to tell you, but one last question—how did you know there would be an earthquake?"

"It was written in the sky," Dennis answered. "In the strange colors. But here's a question for you, then I'll leave you to rest until we arrive at port. Did you really talk to a kushtaka?"

I sighed and said, "I don't know, Dennis. I really don't know."

EPILOGUE

After a few days in Yakutat, fed and clothed by the Tlingit, I was able to hitch a ride on a float plane that had come in from Anchorage to deliver supplies.

I was quiet for the entire 300 mile trip, thinking about the only other float plane trip I'd ever taken, the one going the other direction, to Lituya Bay.

I wasn't sure if part of the events during my stay on Cenotaph Island hadn't been a starvation-induced dream, but in any case, it had turned out for the better, as I no longer had any desire to die.

Back in Anchorage, I tried to call my kids, but had no luck, and I wasn't sure they would want to see me anyway. I then called my aunt and uncle in Tucson, who said they would wire me enough money to get back to the Lower 48.

It was then that I realized I wouldn't be able to collect the money, as I had no ID. I called the motor vehicle people, but they said I had to have some form of ID to get a new license.

It was a Catch 22, and I ended up borrowing a few hundred from an old friend, who also let me sleep on his couch for a few nights. He said he barely recognized me when he came to pick me up at the airport.

While at his place, I tried everything I could to get a new ID, but it was hopeless. It would take weeks to get a birth certificate, and I couldn't abuse the hospitality of my friend that long, nor could I prove residence, since I didn't have one.

I'd truly become Nemo, nobody.

I then had my friend take me to my old house while my ex was at work, hoping against hope that Max would be there.

I'll never forget my trepidation when I opened the back gate and called his name. I didn't know what I would do if he was gone.

But there he was, thin and unkempt, but so happy to see me that I knew things would be OK. All that mattered was that I had Max back.

As we pulled away in my friend's car, Max in the back, I had one last look at my old life. I felt nothing.

I had decided to go back to Utah, but it now didn't look like I was going anywhere. There was no way I could fly without an ID, and even if I were somehow able to get a ride, I couldn't cross into Canada. I was stuck in Alaska.

Finally, I called Dennis and asked if he could somehow help me. We'd become friends, and he eventually joined me later in Utah to help build my house.

Dennis knew someone with a halibut boat who needed hands. The boat would deliver its catch to Seattle, and I could get off there. It was a way to earn some money and also get away from Alaska. Having a dog was a bit question-able, but they thought it might work.

It was a long journey, and I ended up making good money on the way. I then hitched to Utah, and I swear that having a dog made the trip easier, as people would feel sorry for Max and pick us up. Even though I now had some money, I didn't know of any other way to get him there. There was no way I would ship him, and I couldn't afford a car.

I soon had a job in Utah working construction. I bought an old pickup and took Max to work with me every day, not wanting to let him out of my sight for one minute. I knew he felt the same way.

In the evenings, we'd go out into the countryside and walk, and I would relish being there—far from Kah Lituya, tsunamis, blue creatures, and land-otter men. It became my new and permanent happy place.

While walking, I'd ponder the many unresolved questions about my time in Lituya Bay.

Had the creature really wanted me dead, or did it simply just want me to leave? Had I really been visited by a land-otter man, or had it been a hallucination? And why hadn't I died like the kushtaka had predicted? Was it all just superstition? Was anything real?

When Dennis came to stay with me for awhile, we had many late-night discussions, and I finally realized I would never have the answers.

My culture wasn't Tlingit—I was a Westerner who'd been thrown into a different world, one I would never comprehend, but that was OK.

But there was one thing we could share, and that was a mutual respect. Through Dennis, I finally learned to trust people again.

We spent many hours fly-fishing in the Uintah Mountains, and even though he'd never fly-fished, he was soon as adept at that as he was with a kayak paddle. He loved trout, calling it mountain salmon.

I eventually started my own construction company and built myself a small house, with Dennis's help.

But after all that time, I still hadn't been able to contact my kids.

But one day, I got an email from Dennis that linked to a story in the *Anchorage Daily News*. It seems that a fisherman had found my tattered jacket and driver's license and had turned it in to the state troopers, thinking I was a missing person.

I had to laugh, as I was missing, but not in the way one might think. But it also made me feel sober, thinking about how very close I'd actually come to being permanently lost.

I knew the probability was good that someone I knew in Alaska had seen the story and told my family, and sure enough, my son Mark got in touch with my aunt and uncle in Tucson to see if they knew anything about my whereabouts.

Mark and I finally reconnected and gradually established a new relationship—in fact, I think he's going to leave Alaska and come work for me. My daughter and I now talk once in awhile by phone.

In any case, when I stop and think about all this, I know I really shouldn't be alive. I guess it's true that you don't know what you're made of until your back's against the wall. They say that sometimes you have to hit rock bottom to test your mettle, and maybe it's true.

I'm not sure if I passed that test or not, but I do know that not a day goes by that I don't think of the blue creature and thank it for waking me up to a better life. It caused something inside me to change—instead of dying, I decided to fight back.

I would like to think that I eventually outwitted the hand of my blackest fears and outsmarted the creature, but I didn't. I was just incredibly lucky, but I did leave Lituya Bay holding tight to life, happy to be alive.

And every year, on the anniversary of my rescue, I send Dennis a small case of smoked rainbow trout. In return, he sends me wild Alaska salmon from his family's smoke house.

Sometimes, when I'm sitting on the back porch with Max, the two of us sharing salmon, a Robert Service poem will come to mind, and I'll smile.

But other times, I think I can hear the wild and terrible howl of the ghost-like blue creature, far far away, and I'm very happy to be where I am.

And I know I'll never return to Lituya Bay.

ABOUT THE AUTHOR

Rusty Wilson is a fly-fishing guide based in Colorado and Montana. He's well-known for his dutch-oven cookouts and campfires, where he's heard some pretty wild stories about the creatures in the woods, especially Bigfoot.

Whether you're a Bigfoot believer or not, we hope you enjoyed this book, and we know you'll enjoy Rusty's many others, the first of which is *Rusty Wilson's Bigfoot Campfire Stories*, as well as his popular *Chasing After Bigfoot: My Search for North America's Most Elusive Creature*.

Rusty's books come in ebook format, as well as in print and audio.

You'll also enjoy the first book in the Bud Shumway mystery series, a Bigfoot mystery, *The Ghost Rock Cafe*.

Other offerings from Yellow Cat Publishing include an RV series by RV expert Sunny Skye, which includes *Living the Simple RV Life*. And don't forget to check out the books by Sunny's friend, Bob Davidson: *On the Road with Joe*, and *Any Road, USA*. And finally, saving the best for last, you'll love Roger Dean Miller's comedy thriller, *Bombing Hoffman*.

Made in United States
Troutdale, OR
09/26/2024

Made in United States
Troutdale, OR
06/29/2024